Hello,
My Name
Is Ruby

PHILIP C. STEAD

A NEAL PORTER BOOK
ROARING BROOK PRESS
NEW YORK

RUBY INTRODUCED HERSELF. "Hello, my name is Ruby."
"Hello," said the bird standing in the cool water.
"Today is a very nice day," said Ruby. She looked up at the blue sky.
"Would you like to come flying?" asked the bird.

"I am glad to meet you," said Ruby, gliding happily along.
Ruby had never flown with a friend before.

"Hello, my name is Ruby. Would you like to come flying?"
"What is flying?" asked the bird.
"Flying is how to get places."

"This is how I get places," said the bird.
"There are so many things to see!" said Ruby.

"Hello, little bird. My name is Ruby."

"Hello, Ruby," said the bird.

"Little bird, are you ever afraid because you are small?"

"Yes," said the bird, "but sometimes I do not feel small.
  Would you like to see?"

Ruby introduced herself . . .

"Hello," she said.

"My name is Ruby."

"Would you like to be my friend?"

"No, thank you."

Ruby sang a sad song.

She sang and sang until the sun came out
and her feathers were dry.

Along came a curious bird.

Ruby tried to be brave. "Hello, my name is Ruby. Do you have a name?"

"What is a name?" asked the bird.

"A name is a sound that is all yours," she said. "Like this . . ."

ROOO-beee, ROOO-beee-OOO-beee-OOO-beee.

SKEEP-wock, replied the bird. *SKEEEEEP-wock-wock-wock.*

"I am glad to meet you, Skeepwock," said Ruby.

"I am glad to meet you, too," said Skeepwock. "I have heard your name before."

"Really?" said Ruby.

"Really," said Skeepwock. And then he showed her.

Ruby introduced herself, "Hello, my name is Ruby."

ROOO-beee-OOO-beee-OOO-beee, sang the birds. "We are glad to meet you."

Ruby floated happily above the treetop. "I am glad to meet you, too!" she said. "I wonder . . ."

"Would you like to meet my friends?"

To Wednesday,
who knows how difficult it can be

Copyright © 2013 by Philip C. Stead

A Neal Porter Book

Published by Roaring Brook Press

Roaring Brook Press is a division of Holtzbrinck Publishing Holdings Limited Partnership

175 Fifth Avenue, New York, New York 10010

mackids.com

Library of Congress Cataloging-in-Publication Data

Stead, Philip Christian.

Hello, my name is Ruby / Philip C. Stead. — First edition.

pages cm

"A Neal Porter Book."

Summary: "Ruby, a very small bird in a very big world, is looking for a friend, so she introduces herself . . ."— Provided by publisher.

ISBN 978-1-59643-809-5 (hardcover : alk. paper)

[1. Birds—Fiction. 2. Friendship—Fiction.] I. Title.

PZ7.S808566Hel 2013

[E]—dc23

2012046929

Roaring Brook Press books may be purchased for business or promotional use.

For information on bulk purchases please contact Macmillan Corporate and Premium Sales Department

at (800) 221-7945 x5442 or by email at specialmarkets@macmillan.com.

First edition 2013

Book design by Philip C. Stead

Printed in China by South China Printing Co. Ltd., Dongguan City, Guangdong Province

1   3   5   7   9   10   8   6   4   2